BIZET

JEUX D'ENFANTS
(Children's Games)

OPUS 22
FOR ONE PIANO, FOUR HANDS

EDITED BY CHARLES TIMBRELL

AN ALFRED MASTERWORK EDITION

Cover art: Blind Man's Buff
by Andre Henri Dargelas (1828–1906)
Phillips, The International Fine Arts Auctioneers, UK
www.bridgeman.com

Music engraving: Greg Plumblee

GEORGES BIZET

Contents

This edition is dedicated to
Jeffrey Chappell, with
admiration.

Charles Timbrell

Jeux d'enfants (Children's Games), Opus 22

Edited by Charles Timbrell

About This Edition

This edition is based on the two primary sources: the autograph, completed in the autumn of 1871 and presently located in the Bibliothèque Nationale, Paris (Ms 454); and the first edition, published in 1872 by Durand, Schoenewerk & Cie, Paris (plate number D.S. et Cie 1365). Reference is also made to a secondary source: Bizet's orchestration of Nos. 2, 3, 6, 11 and 12, published posthumously in 1882 as *Petite suite d'orchestre*, Op. 22 by Durand, Schoenewerk & Cie, Paris. No sketches or corrected proofs are known to exist.

This edition is based primarily on the first edition, for it includes revisions and corrections that postdate the autograph. The metronome markings, which appear in the first edition but not in the autograph, are presumably Bizet's. Bizet's few pedal indications are identified in footnotes. Although the first edition gives these pedal indications for both players, this editor has placed all pedal in the *secondo* part. All other pedal markings (not directly attributed to Bizet) are editorial. Likewise, all fingerings and redistributions are editorial unless otherwise indicated. All parenthetical material is editorial. Obvious errors (such as missing ties or accidentals) are corrected in the score without parentheses.

Background

Bizet dedicated *Jeux d'enfants* to "Mesdemoiselles Marguerite de Beaulieu et Fanny Gouin." Although nothing certain is known about these two women, Bizet's dedication is worth noting because it explains why the parts were identified as *prima* and *seconda* (feminine gender) in the autograph and first edition. They have been changed to the standard *primo* and *secondo* in this edition. There is no information about the first performance.

It is interesting to note the evolution of *Jeux d'enfants*. The original version consisted of 10 pieces. In the published version, the first four pieces were placed in a different order, Nos. 2 and 6 were re-titled, and two more pieces—Nos. 7 and 8—were added, probably at the publisher's request.

Original Version:

No. 1 – *Les chevaux de bois*
No. 2 – *La poupée*
No. 3 – *La toupie d'Allemagne*
No. 4 – *L'escarpolette*
No. 5 – *Le volant*
No. 6 – *Les soldats de plomb*
No. 7 – *Colin-maillard*
No. 8 – *Saute-mouton*
No. 9 – *Petit mari, petite femme!*
No. 10 – *Le bal*

Published Version (including subtitle and translation):

No. 1 – *L'escarpolette (Rêverie)*; The Swing
No. 2 – *La toupie (Impromptu)*; The Top
No. 3 – *La poupée (Berceuse)*; The Doll
No. 4 – *Les chevaux de bois (Scherzo)*; The Merry-go-round
No. 5 – *Le volant (Fantaisie)*; The Shuttlecock
No. 6 – *Trompette et tambour (Marche)*; Trumpet and Drum
No. 7 – *Les bulles de savon (Rondino)*; Soap Bubbles
No. 8 – *Les quatre coins (Esquisse)*; Puss in the Corner
No. 9 – *Colin-maillard (Nocturne)*; Blindman's Buff
No. 10 – *Saute-mouton (Caprice)*; Leapfrog
No. 11 – *Petit mari, petite femme! (Duo)*;
           Little Husband, Little Wife!
No. 12 – *Le bal (Galop)*; The Dance

Bizet's arrangement of five of the pieces for orchestra was published as *Petite suite d'orchestre*, Op. 22. It was premiered in Paris at the Théâtre de l'Odéon on March 2, 1873, with Edouard Colonne conducting. In this version, Bizet reversed the titles and subtitles of the pieces from the published piano version, thinking that the original titles were too juvenile for an orchestral work. The order and orchestration of the pieces are given below.

Petite suite d'orchestre, Op. 22:

No. 1 – *Marche (Trompette et tambour)*: piccolo, flute, 2 oboes, 2 clarinets, 2 bassoons, 4 horns, 2 trumpets, 2 timpani, triangle, drum, cymbals, strings

No. 2 – *Berceuse (La poupée)*: double winds (2 flutes, 2 oboes, 2 clarinets, 2 bassoons), 2 horns, muted strings

No. 3 – *Impromptu (La toupie)*: double winds, 4 horns, 2 trumpets, 2 timpani

No. 4 – *Duo (Petit mari, petite femme!)*: strings alone

No. 5 – *Galop (Le bal)*: double winds, 4 horns, 2 trumpets, 2 timpani, strings

Bizet and the Piano

An only child, Georges Bizet (1838–1875) was greatly influenced by the musicians in his family. His father was a singing teacher and sometime composer, his mother was a talented pianist, and her brother was a noted singing teacher. At age nine he was admitted to the Paris Conservatoire, where he studied piano with Antoine-François Marmontel (1816–1898), an influential teacher whose later students included Isaac Albéniz (1860–1909), Louis Diémer (1843–1919) and Edward MacDowell (1860–1908). He also studied fugue and counterpoint with Pierre Zimmerman (1785–1853) and Charles Gounod (1818–1893). In 1851 he was awarded a second prize in piano and in the following year he won a first prize playing Henri Herz's (1803–1888) Piano Concerto No. 3. In 1853 he entered the composition class of Fromental Halévy (1799–1862), whose daughter he was to marry. He received first prizes in fugue and organ two years later.

In 1857 Bizet was awarded the Prix de Rome, which allowed him to live in Italy for three years. Here he composed a *Te Deum* (1858) and an opera, *Don Procopio* (1859), as well as a number of unfinished works. His most important later works, all composed in Paris, include the opera *Les pêcheurs de perles* (1863), the orchestral suite *L'arlésienne* (1872) and his masterpiece, the opera *Carmen* (1874). He died prematurely on June 3, 1875 at age 36. His funeral, two days later, was attended by 4,000 people. That evening, the Opéra-Comique presented a performance of *Carmen* as a memorial.

Bizet was a brilliant pianist and a highly skilled sight reader. His keyboard accomplishments were praised by many of his contemporaries, including Hector Berlioz (1803–1869) and Franz Liszt (1811–1886). He shied away from public performance, however, and was heard mainly in salons and at charity events. He was commissioned to write numerous piano reductions of operas (which may have impeded his development of an idiomatic style of writing for solo piano). Except for *Jeux d'enfants*, his piano works remain largely unknown. They include: *Trois esquisses musicales* (1858); *Venise* (1865); *Chasse fantastique* (1866); *Chants du Rhin* (1866); *Variations chromatiques* (1868); *Marine* (1868); and *Nocturne in D* (1868).

The *Variations chromatiques* display much originality and are worthy of investigation by today's pianists. The earlier pieces seem to be closely modeled on works by Liszt and Robert Schumann (1810–1856).

About the Music

Jeux d'enfants, Bizet's last and finest piano work, is one of the gems of piano duet literature. Its 12 colorful pieces describe various children's activities, much in the spirit of Schumann's *Kinderscenen* (1838). Even though the music is often too advanced to be played by children, its charming simplicity and directness appeal to all who are young or young at heart. The basic requirements for both players are lightness of touch, control of a wide variety of dynamics, quick reflexes, and always a keen sense of humor.

Except in the first piece, Bizet gives few indications for the damper pedal. In general, a transparent sound should be maintained, even when the dynamic is forte. Bizet's indications for the una corda pedal should be seriously considered—and perhaps supplemented—due to the increased sonority of modern grand pianos and the possibility that the *secondo* part might overwhelm the *primo* part. As always, these decisions will depend on the instrument used and the acoustics of the performing space.

The *secondo* player must provide absolutely precise rhythmic underpinning throughout the work and a very discreet touch in Nos. 3 ("as *pp* as possible"), 7, 9 and 11. Both players should exploit the quieter range of dynamics to honor Bizet's frequent indications of *ppp*, *pp* and *p*. Even when Bizet indicates *ff* (as in Nos. 4, 6, 8, 10 and 12), it is only for a brief section. Bizet specifically requests rapid *leggiero* playing in Nos. 2, 5, 6, 7, 10 and 12; both players need to feel comfortable with this light-touch technique.

Ensemble problems tend to occur especially in Nos. 5, 8 and 10. In these pieces, and perhaps others, it would be wise to occasionally practice a simplification of the parts to ensure precise ensemble. For example, in No. 5, the players might practice playing only the 32d notes throughout. On the other hand, some pieces (including Nos. 2, 4, 6 and 12) will almost "play themselves" once the parts are learned.

When Bizet indicates *espressivo*, a bit of rubato might be in order. Generally, however, it suffices to play quite strictly except where he indicates smorzando, calando, ritardando or allargando.

Cues must be rehearsed carefully, especially for Nos. 2, 6, 7 and 8, where the players begin together. In these cases, one player should act as "leader," subtly providing a predetermined number of beats before playing. This might be achieved by up-and-down movements of the hand on a key, a discreet movement of the head, a rhythmic intake of breath, or a whispered count. Pacing is an important element in an effective performance of this work; it seems best to separate the pieces by only a few seconds of silence. It is interesting to note that Bizet indicates fermatas only after Nos. 1 and 7, both of which are followed by very rapid pieces. The total performance time (following Bizet's metronome indications) is about 21 minutes. Performance of a selection of the pieces can also be effective, as Bizet's own truncation for orchestra demonstrates.

The following suggestions may help to stimulate the players' imaginations:

No. 1 – *L'escarpolette (Rêverie)*; The Swing: The arpeggios rise and fall, describing the movement of a swing that the children cause to go higher and higher (note the modulation from G to A-flat) before allowing it to slow down and finally stop. The subtitle *Rêverie* suggests a mood of carefree daydreaming.

No. 2 – *La toupie (Impromptu)*; The Top: A top spins at high speed, winds down, falls on its side, and is started again. The subtitle *Impromptu* suggests that the tempo changes should sound spontaneous.

No. 3 – *La poupée (Berceuse)*; The Doll: A young girl rocks her doll to sleep while singing a lullaby.

No. 4 – *Les chevaux de bois (Scherzo)*; The Merry-go-round: The wooden horses seem to gallop at a fast speed while the young riders have great fun.

No. 5 – *Le volant (Fantaisie)*; The Shuttlecock: In a game of badminton, players bat the shuttlecock back and forth with such skill that it never hits the ground.

No. 6 – *Trompette et tambour (Marche)*; Trumpet and Drum: The marchers move with utmost precision, stepping high to the beat of the drum and the fanfares of the trumpet. They retreat into the distance at the end of their demonstration.

No. 7 – *Les bulles de savon (Rondino)*; Soap Bubbles: The carefree children blow evanescent, dancing bubbles.

No. 8 – *Les quatre coins (Esquisse)*; Puss in the Corner: In this game, four children are positioned in the four corners of a room, with a fifth one in the middle. At a given signal, each rushes to a different corner, and the one who fails to secure a corner assumes the middle position for the next round.

No. 9 – *Colin-maillard (Nocturne)*; Blindman's Buff: The blindfolded child stumbles and gropes about before finally capturing and identifying a playmate. The subtitle *Nocturne* is possibly a musical reference to the darkness behind the blindfold.

No. 10 – *Saute-mouton (Caprice)*; Leapfrog: The pianists' hands leap over one another with the agility of children playing "leapfrog."

No. 11 – *Petit mari, petite femme! (Duo)*; Little Husband, Little Wife!: The children play at being a contented husband and wife. A slight disagreement seems to take place at measures 57–75, but it is followed by forgiveness and even a brief and tender duet (measures 82 to the end).

No. 12 – *Le bal (Galop)*; The Dance: The children join in a rousing *galop*, a fast dance of German origin in $\frac{2}{4}$ time.

Bibliography

Curtiss, Mina. *Bizet and His World*. New York: Knopf, 1958.

Dean, Winton. *Bizet*. London: Dent, 1975.

Macdonald, Hugh. "Bizet," *The New Grove II*. London: Macmillan, 2001.

Pigot, Charles. *Georges Bizet et son oeuvre*. Paris: C. Delagrave, 1911.

L'ESCARPOLETTE
(The Swing)

SECONDO

Georges Bizet
(1838–1875)
Op. 22, No. 1

ⓐ Maintain a careful balance with the primo part in measures 1–9 and 45–62.

ⓑ Bizet's pedal and *una corda* indication.

ⓒ Bizet's *tre corde* indication.

ⓓ The melody should sing prominently over the primo part until measure 45.

L'ESCARPOLETTE
(The Swing)

PRIMO

Georges Bizet
(1838–1875)
Op. 22, No. 1

RÊVERIE
Andantino, ♪ = 144

SECONDO

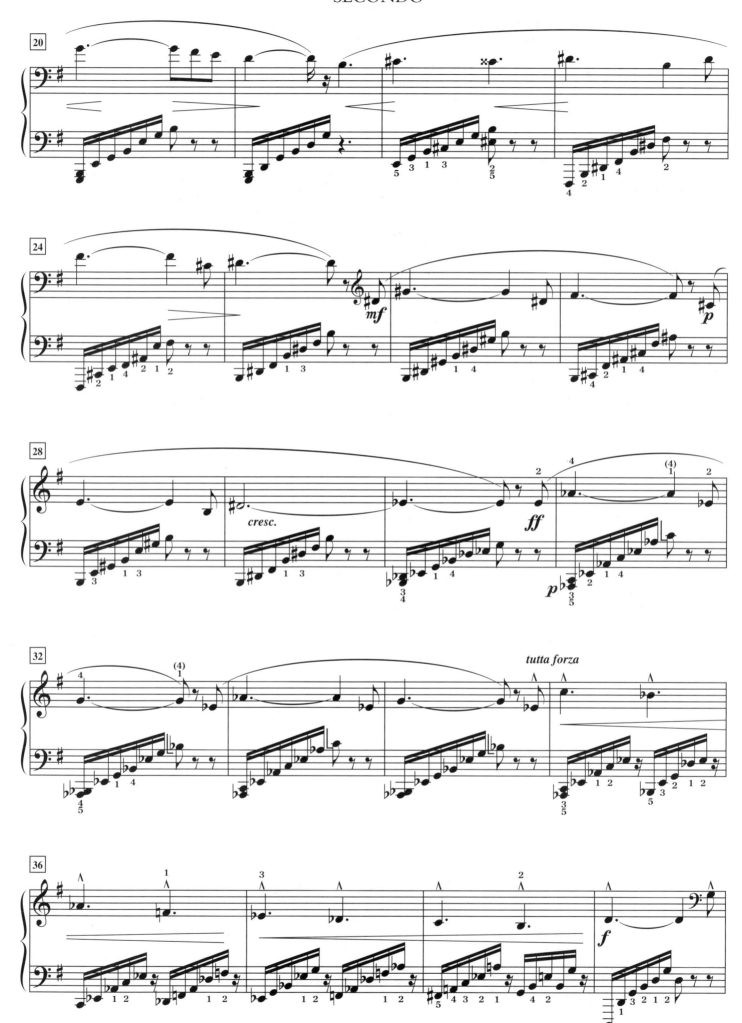

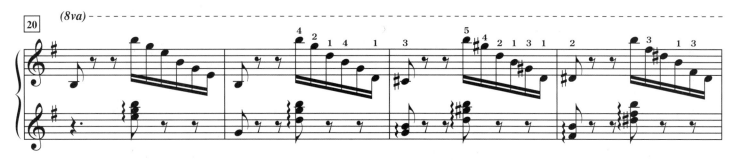

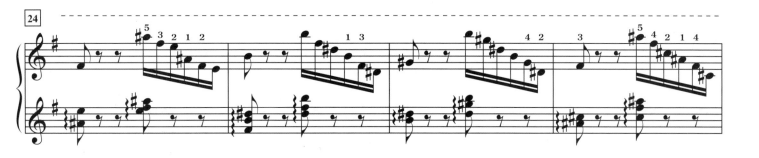

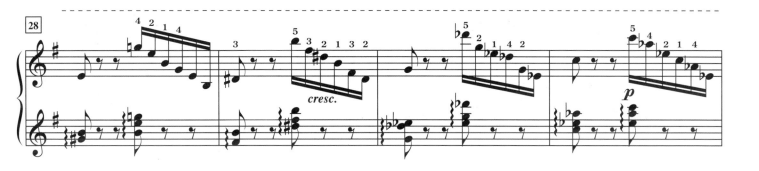

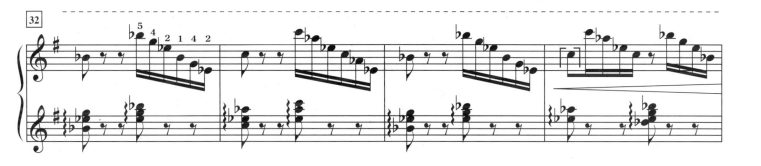

(e) Bizet's pedal.

(f) Bizet's *una corda* indication.

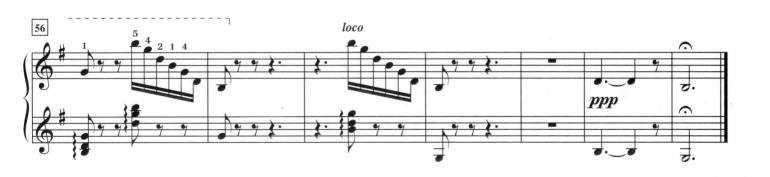

LA TOUPIE
(The Top)

SECONDO

Georges Bizet
(1838–1875)
Op. 22, No. 2

(a) In this piece, the secondo part is the more difficult one. Keep the fingers close to the keys to help assure absolute rhythmic precision and dynamic control at the required speed.

(b) The short diminuendo sign (in measures 13 and 49) is missing in the autograph but is present in the first edition.

(c) Although the autograph and first edition are marked "2 Ped" (that is, *deux pedales,* or both pedals) for measures 28–30 and 64–66, this editor believes that the *una corda* pedal might be extended to include measures 28–37 and 64–71.

La toupie
(The Top)

PRIMO

Georges Bizet
(1838–1875)
Op. 22, No. 2

ⓐ The redistribution in measures 1–3, 37–38 and 71–72 helps to assure good ensemble and a well-controlled diminuendo in the first two instances.

ⓓ The fingering in measures 31–33 and 67– 70 is Bizet's (except those in parentheses).

PRIMO

ⓑ The fingering in measures 34–36 and 67–70 is Bizet's (except those in parentheses).

LA POUPÉE
(The Doll)

SECONDO

Georges Bizet
(1838–1875)
Op. 22, No. 3

(a) All *una corda* and *tre corde* indications in this piece are Bizet's.

(b) In the first edition, *pochissimo sf* appears in measure 10, but it is not present in the autograph. This edition follows the autograph in this instance. *Pochissimo sf* is found in both sources at measure 26, where this editor retains the indication because of the thickened texture.

(c) All pedal markings in this piece are Bizet's.

LA POUPÉE
(The Doll)

PRIMO

Georges Bizet
(1838–1875)
Op. 22, No. 3

BERCEUSE
Andantino semplice, ♪ = 136

pp *naïvement*
(naively)

pp

cresc.

dim.

pp

ppp

p

croisez (cross LH over)

(a) In the first edition, *pochissimo sf* appears in measure 10, but it is not present in the autograph. This edition follows the autograph in this instance. *Pochissimo sf* is found in both sources at measure 26, where this editor retains the indication because of the thickened texture.

(b) Although the right-hand G-natural is tied in the first edition, this editor has omitted the tie to match the music in measure 31.

SECONDO

PRIMO

LES CHEVAUX DE BOIS
(The Merry-go-round)

SECONDO

Georges Bizet
(1838–1875)
Op. 22, No. 4

ⓐ Avoid stressing beat four throughout this piece.

ⓑ In the first edition, the **p** is placed on beat one of measures 5, 25 and 29.

ⓒ Bizet's fingering in measures 7 and 8.

LES CHEVAUX DE BOIS
(The Merry-go-round)

PRIMO

Georges Bizet
(1838–1875)
Op. 22, No. 4

ⓐ Avoid stressing beat four throughout this piece.

SECONDO

ⓓ Bizet's fingering in measures 39–40 and 46–47.

ⓔ All pedal markings in this piece are Bizet's.

ⓕ In the autograph and first edition, the chord lacks an A.

(b) In the first edition, the *f* appears on beat one of measure 37.

(g) In the autograph and first edition, the pedal in measures 80 and 84 is released just before the sixth beat. This editor believes this seems too late, given the decrescendo.

(h) A crescendo is missing in both sources (compare with measure 79).

(i) In the autograph, the *p* appears at the end of measure 84 (but not at the end of measure 80).

(j) For a soft, fast, on-the-keys tremolo, raise the wrist and turn the hand slightly to the left.

© A crescendo is missing in both sources (compare with measure 79).

LE VOLANT
(The Shuttlecock)

SECONDO

Georges Bizet
(1838–1875)
Op. 22, No. 5

ⓐ The chords must be very light and always balanced and synchronized carefully with the primo part.

ⓑ Bizet's fingering throughout; editorial fingering is in parentheses.

ⓒ Measures 13–16 and 21–28 must be rhythmically and tonally precise.

LE VOLANT
(The Shuttlecock)

PRIMO

Georges Bizet
(1838–1875)
Op. 22, No. 5

(a) The scale figures should be very light and unaccented, carefully balanced with the secondo part.

(b) Bizet's fingering throughout; editorial fingering is in parentheses.

(c) Measures 13–16 and 21–28 must be rhythmically and tonally precise.

SECONDO

TROMPETTE ET TAMBOUR
(Trumpet and Drum)

SECONDO

Georges Bizet
(1838–1875)
Op. 22, No. 6

MARCHE
Allegretto mouvᵗ de marche, ♩ = 132

toujours détaché
(always detached)

(a) This dynamic marking is editorial (Bizet gave no indication for the first note).

(b) An accent appears here in the first edition. (This editor believes this was most likely an error.)

(c) Dynamics in measures 21–24 are missing in the autograph.

Trompette et Tambour
(Trumpet and Drum)

PRIMO

Georges Bizet
(1838–1875)
Op. 22, No. 6

MARCHE
Allegretto mouv.^t de marche, ♩ = 132

ⓐ This dynamic marking is editorial (Bizet gave no indication for the first note).

ⓑ Dynamics in measures 21–24 are missing in the autograph.

SECONDO

(d) A very slight ritardando is effective on the last two beats here (in both parts) as well as in measure 53.

(e) The autograph contains alternate versions of measure 26 forward. This edition follows the final version in the first edtition.

(f) Measures 30–33 contain Bizet's fingering (except those in parentheses).

(g) The left-hand accent is missing in the first edition (also in measure 37).

PRIMO

© A very slight ritardando is effective on the last two beats here (in both parts) as well as in measure 53.

ⓓ Hold the right-hand note as long as possible, or take it with the left hand.

ⓔ The autograph contains alternate versions of measure 26 forward. This edition follows the final version in the first edition.

ⓕ The fingering in measures 32–33 and 36–37 is Bizet's.

SECONDO

ⓗ For a soft, fast, on-the-keys tremolo, raise the wrist and arm and turn the hand slightly to the left.

LES BULLES DE SAVON
(Soap Bubbles)

SECONDO

Georges Bizet
(1838–1875)
Op. 22, No. 7

(a) The first edition has a crescendo here; however, this is most likely an error (compare to the primo part, measures 5–6).

LES BULLES DE SAVON
(Soap Bubbles)

PRIMO

Georges Bizet
(1838–1875)
Op. 22, No. 7

SECONDO

ⓑ No ritardando to the end.

ⓒ This editor believes that the marcato should be ignored, in light of the **pp** dynamic marking.

ⓐ No ritardando to the end.

ⓑ This editor believes that the marcatos (in measures 34–35) should be ignored, in light of the **pp** dynamic marking.

LES QUATRE COINS
(Puss in the Corner)

SECONDO

Georges Bizet
(1838–1875)
Op. 22, No. 8

ⓐ All pedal markings between measures 27 and 56 are editorial.

ⓑ The first edition indicates *pp* instead of *p*; this edition follows the autograph, reserving *pp* for measures 34 forward.

LES QUATRE COINS
(Puss in the Corner)

PRIMO

Georges Bizet
(1838–1875)
Op. 22, No. 8

SECONDO

ⓒ The autograph lacks the slurs that are present in the first edition.

(a) The first edition indicates **mf** instead of **f**; this edition follows the autograph.

SECONDO

ⓓ This editor believes that a slight relaxation of the tempo is effective in measures 87–96.

ⓔ Pedal markings in measures 87–90 and 132–135 are Bizet's.

ⓑ This editor believes that a slight relaxation of the tempo is effective in measures 87–96.

ⓒ This crescendo mark is present in the autograph but missing in the first edition.

SECONDO

(f) Pedal markings between measures 144 and 149 are editorial.

(g) Pedal markings in measure 153 forward are Bizet's.

COLIN-MAILLARD
(Blindman's Buff)

SECONDO

Georges Bizet
(1838–1875)
Op. 22, No. 9

NOCTURNE
Andante non troppo quasi andantino, ♩ = 68

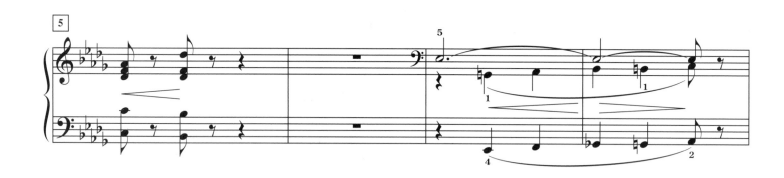

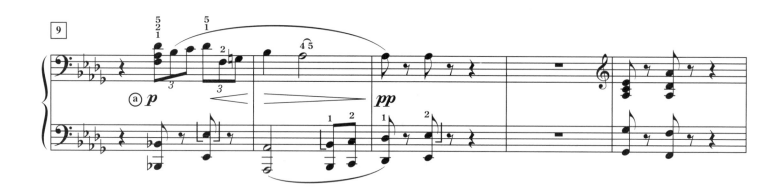

ⓐ The **p** is present in the autograph but missing in the first edition.

COLIN-MAILLARD
(Blindman's Buff)

PRIMO

Georges Bizet
(1838–1875)
Op. 22, No. 9

NOCTURNE
Andante non troppo quasi andantino, ♩ = 68

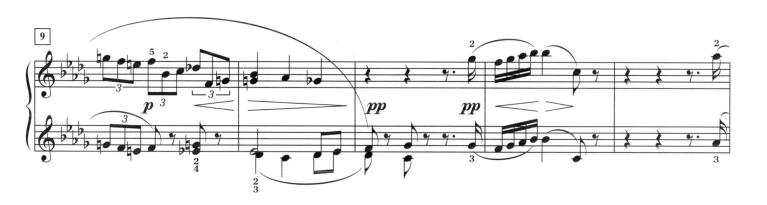

ⓑ The *sf* is present in the autograph but missing in the first edition.

ⓒ The pedal marking in measure 31 is Bizet's. Subsequent pedal markings are editorial.

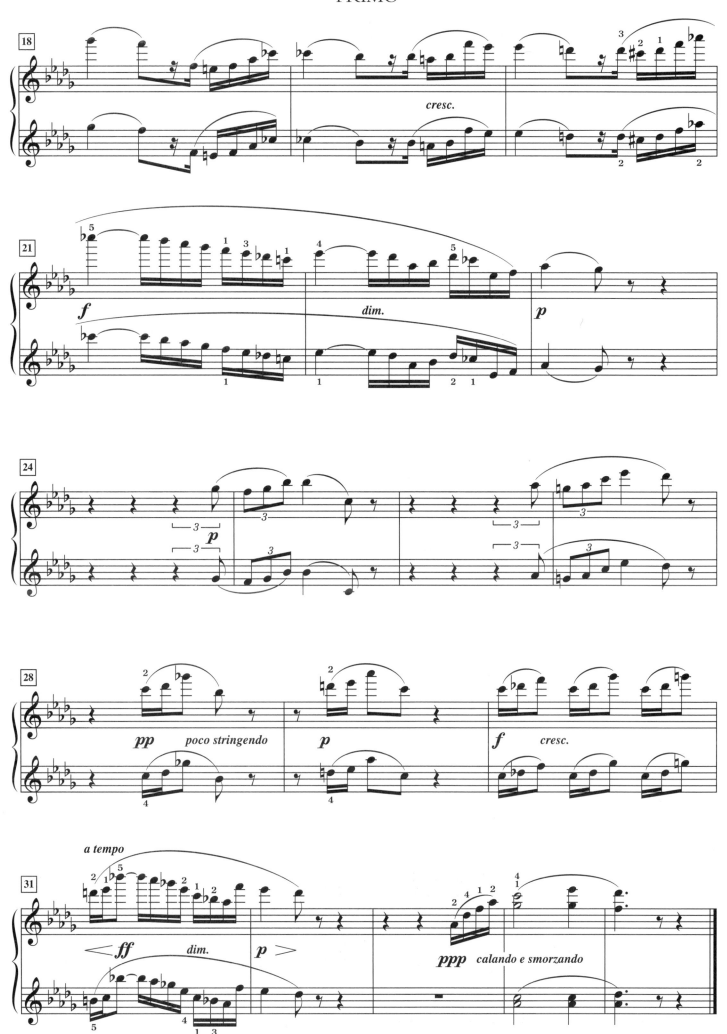

SAUTE-MOUTON
(Leapfrog)

SECONDO

Georges Bizet
(1838–1875)
Op. 22, No. 10

CAPRICE

Allegro molto moderato, ♩ = 116

ⓐ The first edition has an erroneous flat before the D on beat 1.

ⓑ The first edition lacks a B in the chord on beat 1.

Saute-Mouton
(Leapfrog)

PRIMO

Georges Bizet
(1838–1875)
Op. 22, No. 10

PRIMO

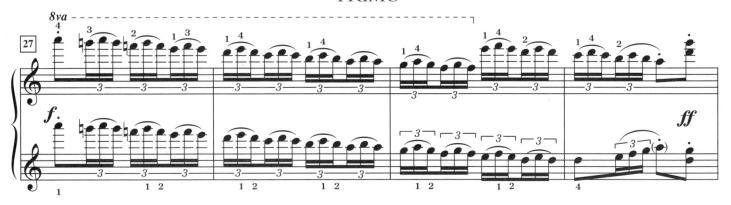

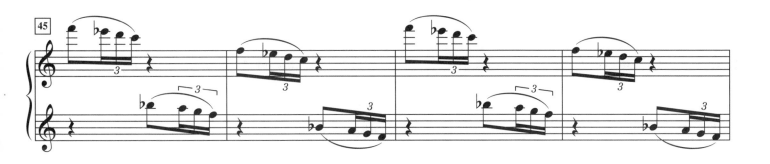

SECONDO

(c) The autograph has a half-note octave in the left hand, changed in the first edition to the present reading.

(d) No ritardando to the end.

(e) Bizet's pedal.

(a) No ritardando to the end.

PETIT MARI, PETITE FEMME!

(Little Husband, Little Wife!)

SECONDO

Georges Bizet
(1838–1875)
Op. 22, No. 11

(a) All notes marked staccato should be lightly detached, discreet, and played close to the keys. Ideally, the *una corda* pedal will not be needed in this piece, except possibly for the final measures.

(b) The *molto espressivo* indication suggests some rubato, but it should be slight. The more pronounced modifications of tempo that occur from measure 43 forward occur in both parts simultaneously.

(c) In measures 17–60, hold all right-hand quarter notes for their full value, lifting the keys only enough to depress them again.

(d) The dynamics for measures 28–42 are missing in the autograph but appear in the first edition.

Petit mari, petite femme!

(Little Husband, Little Wife!)

Georges Bizet
(1838–1875)
Op. 22, No. 11

PRIMO

(a) The *molto espressivo* indication suggests some rubato, but it should be slight. The more pronounced modifications of tempo that occur from measure 43 forward occur in both parts simultaneously.

(b) Play the grace notes before the beat here and in measure 84.

(c) All notes marked staccato should be lightly detached, discreet, and played close to the keys. The left-hand chords in measures 7–17 should perfectly match the sound of the secondo's right-hand chords in measures 1–6.

(d) In measures 18 forward, hold all left-hand quarter notes for their full value, lifting the keys only enough to depress them again.

(e) The dynamics for measures 28–42 are missing in the autograph but appear in the first edition.

(e) Bizet's pedal.

(f) This editor suggests omitting the top note of this chord (it is a melodic note in the primo part).

(g) At measure 85, the first edition has an *a tempo* indication. In light of the *smorzando e calando*, this editor has omitted the *a tempo* and follows the autograph here.

At measure 85, the first edition has an *a tempo* indication. In light of the *smorzando e calando,*
this editor has omitted the *a tempo* and follows the autograph here.

LE BAL
(The Dance)

SECONDO

Georges Bizet
(1838–1875)
Op. 22, No. 12

(a) The *sf* in measures 4 and 12 should be within the context of the prevailing ***pp*** dynamic.

(b) The secondo part should not overwhelm the primo in measures 17–32, 93–108 and 141 to the end.

LE BAL
(The Dance)

PRIMO

Georges Bizet
(1838–1875)
Op. 22, No. 12

(a) The *sf* in measures 4 and 12 should be within the context of the prevailing *pp* dynamic.

(b) The crescendo in measure 15 is missing in the autograph and first edition
(an oversight since the crescendo appears here in the secondo part).

SECONDO

© Keep the hands close to the keys for the rapid repeated chords in measures 49–56 and 125–146.

ⓒ Keep the hands close to the keys for the rapid repeated chords in measures 49–56, 125–126 and 129–130.

(d) The left-hand accents in measures 75 and 79 are missing in the autograph but are present in the first edition.

SECONDO

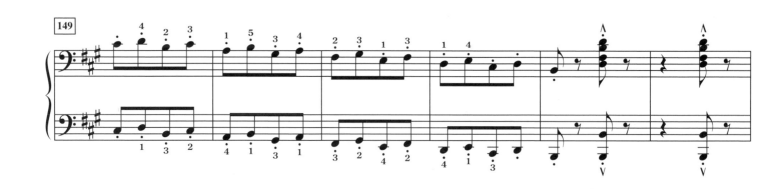

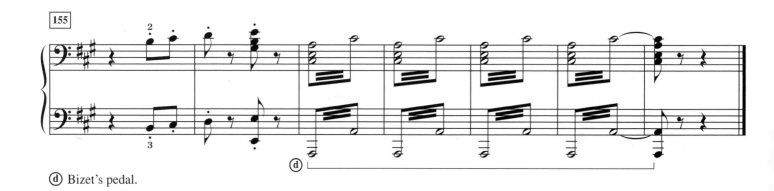

ⓓ Bizet's pedal.